D1013377

Tea for Two

by Melody Mews illustrated by Ellen Stubbings

LITTLE SIMON
New York London Toronto Sydney New Delhi

LITTLE SIMON
An imprint of Simon & Schuster Children's Publishing Division
1230 Avenue of the Americas, New York, New York 10020
First Little Simon paperback edition November 2021.
Designed by Laura Roode. The text of this book was set in Banda.
Manufactured in the United States of America 0522 MTN 10 9 8 7 6 5 4 3 2
Library of Congress Cataloging-in-Publication Data
Names: Mews, Melody, author. | Stubbings, Ellen, illustrator. Title: Tea for two / by Melody Mews ; illustrated by Ellen Stubbings. Description: First Little Simon paperback edition. | New York : Little Simon, 2021. | Series: Itty Bitty Princess Kitty ; 9 | Audience: Ages 5-9. | Audience: Grades K-1. | Summary: Excited over meeting some pegasuses, Itty does not immediately notice that her best friend Luna Unicorn feels lefto ut. Identifi ers: LCCN 2021007788 (print) | LCCN 2021007789 (ebook) | ISBN 9781534487208 (paperback) | ISBN 9781534487215 (hardcover) | ISBN 9781534487222 (ebook)
Subjects: CYAC: Friendship—Fiction. | Cats—Fiction. | Princesses—Fiction. | Unicorns—Fiction.
Classification: LCC PZ7.1.M4976 Te 2021 (print) | LCC PZ7.1.M4976 (ebook) | DDC [Fic]—dc23
LC record available at https://lccn.loc.gov/2021007788 LC ebook record available at https://lccn.loc.gov/2021007789

Contents

chapter 1
RUMBLE

A Fairy Berry Dilemma

Itty Bitty Princess Kitty was in her climbing room when her tummy rumbled. Itty paused. She was practicing high jumps and didn't want to stop for a snack. Her tummy rumbled again. *It* didn't care that she wanted to keep playing.

Itty jumped down and ran toward the kitchen. Until recently, she hadn't been allowed inside while the food fairies were cooking.

But the head food fairy, Garbanzo, had relaxed her rules and *sometimes* allowed Itty to come in. Itty hoped this was one of those times.

"Hi, Peaches." Itty waved to a fairy wearing a chef's hat.

Peaches looked a bit worried. "Hi, Princess. Garbanzo isn't in the best mood. . . ."

"It's okay," Itty replied. "I only want a snack."

Just then, Garbanzo's squeaky but loud voice echoed through the kitchen.

"Where are the ruby red raspberries?" Garbanzo yelled.

"We ran out," a nervous-looking fairy responded.

"Well, that is *fairy* terrible!" Garbanzo stomped her tiny feet. "I was planning to make the King's favorite ruby red raspberry cake!"

Garbanzo's ruby red raspberry cake was not just the King's favorite—it was Itty's favorite too! Just thinking about it made Itty's tummy rumble so loudly that Garbanzo heard it.

"Oh, Princess Itty!" Garbanzo cried, noticing her. "You need to leave—"

"I can help!" Itty said quickly. And she kept talking before Garbanzo could shoo her away. "I'll get you all the berries you need!"

"I can't ask you to do that!" Garbanzo squeaked. "The berries are found at Pegasus Pines and that's *fairy* far away."

"That's close to Starfish Falls and I'm going there anyway for a playdate with Luna," Itty said.

This wasn't exactly true . . . but Itty was sure Luna would be up for it.

"Well, okay then," Garbanzo said. "If you insist."

"Oh, I do insist," Itty said, nodding her head. "How many berries do you need? A bucketful?"

Garbanzo shook her head. "More like ten buckets!"

chapter 2

Pegasus Pines

"Ten buckets?" Luna repeated what Itty had just said. "Do you mean fairy-size buckets?"

"Nope." Itty shook her head. "Garbanzo needs ten *regular*-size buckets of berries. So, will you help me?"

"Of course I will!" Luna exclaimed, glitter spraying from her horn.

Luna Unicorn was Itty's best friend. Itty loved that Luna was always up for an adventure. Itty also loved that Luna's horn spouted glitter when she was excited—except when they were indoors. Trying to get glitter out of a carpet was not easy.

"I've never been to Pegasus Pines," Itty said as they hailed a cloud.

"Me either," said Luna. "But I *have* heard that the best berries in Lollyland grow there."

Soon their cloud parked in a sunny pasture. Itty and Luna hopped off and began unloading their buckets.

"Please stay parked here," Itty told the cloud.

"Itty, look! I think those are ruby red raspberry bushes!" Luna cried, pointing to a cluster of bushes with shiny red berries.

The girls rushed over. Itty popped one of the berries into her mouth. Perfectly ripe and ruby red . . . it was delicious!

"Itty, save some berries for Garbanzo," Luna said as Itty shoved pawfuls of berries into her mouth.

"Sorry," Itty replied with a smile. "I missed snack time."

The girls got to work, picking berries and carrying buckets back to their cloud.

Itty was carrying the tenth and final bucket when she heard a rustling sound. She wondered if there were berry fairies around. Were she and Luna about to get in trouble for picking the fruit?

"Hello!" someone shouted.

Itty was so startled that she dropped her entire bucket of berries!

chapter 3

Hello, Arlo

"I'm so sorry!"

Just then Itty realized it wasn't a fairy. It was a pegasus! The pegasus rushed over to pick up the spilled berries.

"It's okay!" Itty smiled. "I'm Itty, by the way."

The pegasus gasped. "You're the Princess of Lollyland!"

Itty nodded. "That's me! What's your name?"

"I'm Arlo," the pegasus answered. "It's an honor to meet you, Princess Itty."

"Please call me Itty," Itty said. "All my friends do."

"I can't believe I'm talking to the Princess of Lollyland," Arlo said as Luna cleared her throat.

"Oops, sorry, this is Luna Unicorn," Itty said.

Luna smiled. "It's nice to meet you."

"You too," Arlo replied. He turned back to Itty. "My sister is not going to believe I met the Princess of Lollyland. . . ."

He trailed off as he noticed Itty picking up the spilled berries. "Oh, let me do that for you, Princess Itty!" he said.

"We can pick them up together," Itty suggested.

It took Itty, Luna, and Arlo only a few minutes to collect the spilled berries. As Itty loaded the bucket onto their cloud, Arlo sighed sadly.

sigh

"I wish you didn't have to leave already," he said. "We're about to have a tea party. Did you know? We have the best tea in Lollyland because we have the best berries!"

“Well . . . we could probably stay a little longer,” Itty replied. She and Luna smiled at each other.

"Wow, that's great!" Arlo said excitedly. "Follow me!" He led the girls to a clearing where a table was set for a tea party. As they took their seats, a tea fairy

fluttered over and filled their cups with a delicious-smelling blue tea.

Itty took a sip, and a smile spread across her face. “Now, that is truly the best tea I’ve ever had!”

chapter 4

Sapphire Blueberries

“That tea is made from sapphire blueberries grown here,” Arlo said proudly. “They’re my favorite.”

“I think they’re my new favorite too,” Itty replied.

She enjoyed her tea for a few more moments, then had a

sudden realization. "Yikes! We should probably leave soon," she told Luna.

"Oh! I think my friends are here!" said Arlo excitedly.

Suddenly the bushes began to quiver and three pegasuses emerged.

Arlo introduced his friends to Itty and Luna. They were Rosie, Dazzle, and Jacob.

"We're perfectly pleased to meet you," said Jacob to Itty.

"So, you liked our tea?" Dazzle asked.

"I loved it," Itty replied. "I'm going to tell the head of the royal kitchen about sapphire blueberries."

"We'll send some back with you!" Rosie cried.

"Oh, that's okay . . . ," Itty began, but Rosie, Dazzle, and Jacob had already dashed off to collect sapphire blueberries for her.

"We're not used to meeting princesses," Arlo said shyly. "But if you come back to visit, I promise we will try harder *not* to treat you like a princess."

"It's a deal," Itty replied.

A little while later Itty realized that the sun was going down. She hadn't heard the mermaids sing the hour the whole time they had been there. Which meant she had no idea what time it was.

"We have to get back to the palace," Itty told the pegasuses. She said goodbye to her new friends and promised to come back soon.

As she returned to the cloud, Itty saw that Luna was already there.

"Didn't you say goodbye to everyone?" Itty asked.

Luna shrugged. "They didn't say goodbye to me!"

Itty frowned. Was Luna offended? Or was she joking? Or was she simply in a hurry to get back?

"Let's go home before Garbanzo sends out the search party fairies!" Itty said with a smile. She was sure everything would be fine when they got back.

chapter 5

Flying Solo

"Was Garbanzo happy with the berries?" Luna asked.

It was the next day and school had just ended. Itty and Luna were waiting outside for their friends Esme Butterfly and Chipper Bunny.

"Only after she stopped being mad I took so long," Itty said with a laugh. "She really liked the sapphire blueberries, too."

"What are sapphire blueberries?" Chipper asked, a bit out of breath. He sometimes got winded trying

to keep up with Esme, who could fly faster than he could hop.

Itty told Chipper and Esme about Pegasus Pines.

"Arlo is so nice," Itty said. "Right, Luna?"

"I guess." Luna shrugged.

Esme sighed. "I've never been to Pegasus Pines," she said dreamily.

"Neither have I," Chipper said.

"We should go!" Itty cried. "What about right now?"

Itty waved her arms to hail a cloud.

"I can't go now," Chipper said. "I have to go help my mom at the bookstore."

"I have spelling homework," Esme added.

A cloud pulled up and Itty hopped on. "Luna?" She scooched over. "Are you coming?"

"Not today," Luna said. "I have to . . . um . . . my sister asked if I would do something with her. But have fun!"

On the ride to Pegasus Pines, Itty thought about Luna's response. Luna didn't seem sure about whatever she and her sister were doing. Was it possible she just didn't want to come with Itty?

The cloud parked and Itty hopped off. She began to look around for Arlo. A moment later he sprang from a berry bush.

"Itty!" he cried. "Welcome back!"

Itty waved. Then she realized there was another pegasus standing behind Arlo. "Hi, I'm Itty!"

"I know who you are, Princess Itty," the pegasus said shyly.

"I told you not to call her that," Arlo said with a sigh. "Sorry, Itty. This is my sister, Ada."

Itty smiled. "You look so much alike!"

"Well, we are twins," Ada said.

"I didn't know your sister was a twin!" Itty exclaimed. "That's neat!"

Suddenly Ada's face fell.

"You didn't tell her about me?" Ada whispered.

"Arlo told me he had a sister," Itty said quickly. "I just didn't know you were *twins*."

From the way Ada was frowning, Itty knew something was wrong.

She just wasn't sure what.

chapter 6

Forgotten Plans

That night, Itty's mom came to her room to tuck her in at bedtime. Itty was exhausted from her busy day, but she still wanted to tell her mom about her visit to Pegasus Pines.

"When I first met Ada—she's Arlo's twin—there was a little

misunderstanding because she thought Arlo hadn't told me about her," Itty explained. "Her feelings were hurt. But she seemed happier by the time I left. They gave me a tour of Pegasus Pines and it was beautiful."

"That's lovely, darling," the Queen purred.

"I'm going back tomorrow," Itty said, yawning. "I want to bring Arlo and Ada some of Garbanzo's cinnamon scones. Hopefully, this time Luna can come."

As Itty started to drift off to sleep, she thought about all the things she'd seen with Arlo and Ada. She couldn't wait to show them to Luna . . . hopefully.

The next day, when Itty asked Luna to go to Pegasus Pines with her, Luna's face fell, just as Ada's had the day before.

"We were supposed to go to Goodie Grove today, remember?" Luna asked.

Itty had not remembered.

"I'm so sorry. I forgot," Itty said. "Can we go another day? Garbanzo baked a special batch of scones for Arlo and his sister and I want to deliver them while they're fresh."

"Okay," Luna said. But Itty could tell she was disappointed.

"Are you sure?" Itty asked. "I really am sorry I forgot."

"I know you are." Luna gave Itty a small smile. "I'm going to go home and get a head start on homework," she said.

"Are you sure you don't want to come with me?" Itty asked. She was glad that Luna understood, but she still felt like she was letting her best friend down.

"No, that's okay," Luna replied. "But let's play together soon, okay?"

"Definitely," Itty promised.

chapter 7

Arlo and Ada

When Itty arrived at Pegasus Pines, she was surprised to see Arlo standing alone.

"Where's Ada?" Itty asked as she hopped off her cloud.

"She couldn't come," Arlo said bluntly.

Itty waited for him to say more, but he didn't. Instead, he pointed to the basket Itty was holding. "What's that?" he asked.

"These," Itty said with a grin, "are Garbanzo's cinnamon scones. I think they will taste extra yummy with your sapphire blueberry tea."

"Thank you so much!" Arlo cried. Itty was glad to see the big smile on his face. "Can I save them for later to share with Ada?"

"Of course!" Itty said. "They're for both of you."

Arlo nodded, but Itty thought he looked a bit sad.

"Is something wrong?" she asked.

"Well . . . ," Arlo began, clearly not sure whether to continue.

"Ada isn't here because she went to Marshmallow Meadows without me to collect snacks for the fireflies." Arlo's shoulders slumped. "We usually go together, but today she wanted to go by herself."

“Why?” Itty asked.

Arlo looked at the ground. “Ada is upset that I’ve been spending so much time with you. She told me I should ask *you* to be my twin sister.”

"What?" Itty cried. "Ada is your twin—not me!"

"I know. But I guess she feels left out, so she's mad."

Itty felt terrible that Arlo and Ada weren't getting along—and it was because of her.

Then Itty had another thought. Was Luna feeling left out too?

Did Luna think Arlo was taking her place—just like Ada thought Itty was taking *her* place?

That wasn't true at all! But how could Itty and Arlo show them?

Just then, Itty had an idea. "It's going to be okay," she promised Arlo. "I think I know how to fix this!"

chapter 8

Tea for Two

The next day during recess, Itty pulled Luna aside. "Can you come over today after school?" Itty asked.

"Aren't you going to Pegasus Pines to see Arlo?" Luna asked.

"Nope." Itty shook her head. "I have something planned for us."

“Oookay . . . ,” Luna said slowly. Then she smiled. “I’d love to!”

A couple hours later, the desks in Itty’s classroom turned violet, and her teacher, Miss Sophia, announced that the school day was over. Itty and Luna sprang from their seats and headed outside to hail a cloud to the palace.

“So, what do you have planned?” Luna asked as their cloud lifted off.

“You’ll see.” Itty smiled.

Soon, the cloud began its descent on the palace lawn.

"What's all that?" Luna asked, pointing to the colorful umbrella, table, and chairs that were set up on the lawn.

"*That's* what I have planned!" Itty cried. "Come see!" She grabbed Luna's hoof and together they ran across the lawn to where Luna's surprise was waiting. A table was set with plates of yummy goodies, teacups, saucers, and lacy napkins. And two chairs awaited them.

"A tea party?" Luna asked as she spotted the beautiful porcelain tea set on the table.

"Tea for two," Itty said. "Just *us*. And look, there are some marshmallow brownies, and some maple candies, and some of

Garbanzo's ruby red raspberry cake, and sapphire blueberry tea, and . . ." Itty paused and looked closely at Luna. She had been talking this whole time. But what did Luna think of it all?

"So . . ." Itty took a deep breath.

"Do you like it?"

“Do I like it?" Luna repeated. "No. I LOVE it!"

From the spray of glitter that came bursting from her horn, Itty knew her tea party for two was doing just what she had hoped: reminding Luna how special she was to Itty.

chapter 9

A Second Chance

"May I pour some tea for you?" Itty asked. Luna nodded and Itty carefully poured some sapphire blueberry tea into Luna's fancy porcelain teacup.

"This really *is* delicious tea," Luna said after taking a sip.

"Try it with some of the cake," Itty said, scooching the ruby red raspberry cake toward Luna.

Luna took Itty's advice and tried a bite of cake, and then a sip of tea. A little poof of glitter sprayed from her horn.

"See?" Itty giggled.

Luna finished her cake and wiped her mouth with the silky napkin.

"Thank you for doing this," Luna said. "I feel so special!"

"You *are* special," Itty told her. "I realized that you might be feeling bad because I was going to Pegasus Pines to see Arlo a lot. I'm sorry if I made you feel left out. I never meant to."

"I did feel left out, but I feel better now," Luna said. She took another sip of tea. "And I guess if you like Pegasus Pines that much, then maybe I should give it another chance."

"Only if you're sure," Itty said as she nibbled on a piece of cake. "But I do think you would really love it there . . . especially the Pegasus Pines racetrack. There are jumps and hoops, and all sorts of cool things!"

Luna smiled. Then she put down her teacup and tilted it to show Itty that it was empty.

"Well, I think we *have* to go back," Luna said with a giggle. "We're out of tea!"

chapter 10

Party in Pegasus Pines!

A few days later, Itty, Luna, Esme, and Chipper headed to Pegasus Pines. Arlo and Ada were waiting in the pasture when their cloud landed. They were not alone—Rosie, Dazzle, and Jacob were there too.

Itty introduced everyone.

"Does your horn really spray glitter?" Ada asked Luna.

Luna nodded.

"Can you show us?" Dazzle asked.

"Can you give me some sapphire blueberry tea?" Luna giggled.

"Right this way!" Ada exclaimed.

Itty watched as her old friends followed her new friends to the clearing for a tea party.

"Does Ada feel better now?" Itty asked Arlo.

"She does," Arlo said happily.

"I took your advice and created a special picnic for the two of us. I told her I was sorry for making her feel left out."

“I’m so glad,” Itty said. She heard laughter and giggles coming from the clearing and realized she and Arlo were missing out on the fun! “Come on,” she said, grabbing Arlo’s hoof. “I think we just missed a Luna glitter shower!”

A little while later, after drinking lots of yummy tea, the pegasuses introduced Itty and her friends to a new game.

"It's called Freeze Dance Party," Ada said. She explained how to play: you danced while the music was playing and then froze the moment the music stopped. The last one to freeze was out.

"That sounds fun. But where will the music come from?" Itty asked.

The pegasuses looked at one another.

“The dance party fairies, of course,” Arlo said, pointing to a tree stump.

And that's when Itty saw it: a group of fairies wearing glittery outfits had set up their teeny instruments and were ready to play!

"You have *dance party* fairies here?" Luna exclaimed.

"Hello? Can we start?" the lead singer fairy squeaked, tapping her foot. "We don't have all day!"

Arlo and Ada nodded. The music began and everyone started dancing.

"You were right, Itty," Luna cried as she boogied down. "I love Pegasus Pines!"

Have a Freeze Dance Party!

1. Gather some friends.

2. Start the music.

3. Everybody dance!

4. Stop the music.

5. FREEZE!

6. The last one to freeze is out.

7. Repeat steps 1–6 until you have a winner!

Here's a sneak peek at Itty's next royal adventure!

It was a beautiful sunny day in Lollyland. Itty Bitty Princess Kitty and Esme Butterfly were playing in the royal garden at the palace where Itty lived.

"Ohh, look at those poppies," Esme called as she fluttered off to admire the bright orange flowers.

In Itty's opinion, the royal garden was one of the prettiest places in Lollyland. And *the best smelling*, Itty thought, as the gentle breeze carried the perfumed scent through the air.

Itty spotted a watering can and decided the sunflowers looked a little thirsty. She picked it up and sprinkled some cool water on them.

"Do you mind?"

Itty gasped.

"Shh! Sunny, that's the *princess* watering us!"

"Whoops, sorry Princess Itty!" the sunflower named Sunny said.

Itty peered closely at the talking sunflowers. It was no surprise to Itty that they *could* talk—many flowers in Lollyland could. But it was a surprise that they had *chosen* to talk, because flowers usually kept to themselves.

"I'm so sorry!" Itty said. "But . . . don't you like being watered?"

"Usually, yes," Sunny said. "But it just rained. And nobody likes a soggy sunflower."